Go Team!

Written and Illustrated by
Stacy Einfalt
Creative Contributor
Bud Collier

This book is dedicated to the following amazing people:

Evan is an actor from Katy, TX with Down Syndrome. His dream to become an actor has come true. His break out role is on the Netflix series Ozark, starring Jason Bateman and Laura Linney. He is a true hero for our kids. He has been an Ambassador for Imbullyfree.org since 2014. His message to kids, "NEVER LET ANYONE SHATTER YOUR DREAMS".

Kate is the Director of Veteran Affairs for Imbullyfree.org. We are so proud of her. She is very shy about all of the medals she has won as an Athlete for U.S. Paralympics. She has the Olympic record for throwing the Disc for North and South Americas, and has 12 gold medals. After she became paralyzed, she did not give up, but continues to inspire our kids world wide.

The season of fall is beginning to settle over the small suburban town of Buddyville. The air is developing a cold, crisp feeling to it. The leaves on the trees are changing into different shades of bright yellow, red and orange.

The children have all returned to school from enjoying their summer break. Bully Bear, who has fondly been nicknamed B.B. by his friends, is feeling anxious as he and his friend Evan arrive at school this morning.

They head right over to the bulletin board, inside the front lobby, to find that Coach Kind posted the list of students that have been chosen to play on this year's football team.

B.B and Evan give each other a high five when they find that their names are included on the list. They are both really excited about the thought of being able to be a part of a team.

As they turned to leave to head to their classroom, their good friend Katie rolled up to them in her wheelchair. "Morning Katie, how are you?" B.B. acknowledged. "I'm a little nervous this morning." Katie said, "I hope my name is up on Ms. PomPom's list for this year's cheerleading squad." B.B., Katie and Evan begin scanning down the list and, to their delight, they found her name.

5

B.B. and Evan threw their hands up in the air with excitement. B.B. shouted, "Congratulations Katie!", as he gave her a BIG BEAR HUG!

While B.B. and Evan were congratulating Katie, a group of girls arrived to check out the list on the bulletin board. When they saw that Katie's name was on the list along with theirs, they turned and began to laugh. "How are you going to cheer with us?" Callie sneered. Sierra chimed in, "Yeah. You can't even stand up." Tears began to roll down Katie's face as the other girls continued to tease her.

B.B. stepped in between and exclaimed, "Stop picking on her! Can't you see you're hurting her feelings? Just because she has a disability doesn't mean she can't be a cheerleader too." Evan added, "She has the most school spirit out of any of us and I think she will be the best cheerleader on the squad this year!" The girls just glared as B.B., Evan and Katie left to go to their classroom.

After school B.B. rushed home. He couldn't wait to tell his parents about his exciting news. As he arrived he ran up the porch steps and burst through the front door. "Guess what!" B.B. exclaimed, "I made it onto the school's football team this year!"

"That's wonderful!" Mama Bear shouted. "Congratulations! We are so proud of you!" Papa Bear said, as he beamed with pride.

That night when B.B. was all nestled in bed fast asleep, he began dreaming about playing in his first football game.

The next morning B.B. awoke to his alarm and jumped out of bed. As he got dressed, he began thinking about going to football practice after school that day. He was so excited. He rushed downstairs and gobbled down his breakfast Mama Bear made for him, then grabbed his backpack and yelled, "Bye Mama, thank you!", as he ran out the door and headed off to school.

As B.B. walked up onto the school grounds he saw some boys crowded around his friend Evan picking on him. Evan's chin quivered as he tried to hold back tears while standing in the middle, being teased by everyone. "You can't be on our team four eyes." Travis said. "Yeah, you'll make us lose for sure, loser!" added Quinn, as the others laughed and giggled.

B.B. walked right into the middle of the group and put his arm around Evan then glared at the other boys and said, "Stop it! That's no way to treat anyone, especially your teammate." The boys all just gave B.B. and Evan dirty looks as they walked away and headed into the school.

Once inside B.B. turned to Evan and said, "Don't worry about them, I believe in you and soon they will too." Evan cracked a smile and said, "Thanks.", as they turned and headed to class.

Finally, it felt like forever until the last bell of the day rang. B.B. met Evan at their lockers so that they could walk to football practice together.

Once arriving at the field, they sat amongst their teammates anxiously awaiting to hear Coach Kind's instructions.

"Good afternoon team!" Coach Kind said, " I have chosen each one of you because I believe you are all GREAT! Just remember that there is no "I" in team. We must all work together so that we all win! Now who's ready to play some football?" A few of the boys sneered over at B.B. and Evan as they threw up their hands and cheered with the rest of the team.

Coach Kind split the team into two groups, one being offense, the other defense, and began teaching them plays. Travis, who was lined up across from Evan, began taunting and teasing him. Quinn chimed in also saying, "Hey four eyes, hope you can see the ball."

B.B. shouted at them, "Why don't you give him a chance and stop picking on him!" Coach Kind blew his whistle when he heard the commotion and called out, "Travis and Quinn, you both need to go sit on the bench until you decide that you will treat your teammates with respect and not bully them!"

The boys grumbled under their breath as they stomped over to the bench and sat down. As they sat there sulking, they watched how the other teammates were giving Evan a chance to participate by passing the ball to him, even though he didn't catch it half the time.

Travis and Quinn noticed that the other kids never picked on or teased Evan, but rather encouraged him by saying, "It's ok Evan, you'll catch it next time!"

While the football team was practicing out on the field, Katie was sitting in her wheelchair just outside the gymnasium debating whether she wanted to join the other girls for cheerleading practice. She was so afraid that they would make fun of her again.

Bella Bear noticed Katie, as she was heading into practice and said, "Hi Katie! Why are you sitting out here? Aren't you going to practice?"

"I don't know Bella.", Katie said, "I'm afraid that the other girls are going to pick on me again." Suddenly Katie and Bella could hear Ms. PomPom calling over to them, "Come on girls, join us, practice is about ready to begin!"

25

Katie left out a big sigh as she and Bella entered the gymnasium. She saw that some of the other girls began to whisper and giggle as she and Bella approached the group.

Ms. PomPom noticed the girl's reactions as well and said, "Girls that is no way to treat each other. Katie has just as much school spirit as the rest of you and deserves to be a part of our squad. Now you need to apologize to her."

The girls began to feel bad as they looked over at Katie and noticed she was crying. They walked over and each gave her a big hug. "We're sorry Katie.", Kailie said. Cassie chimed in, "Yeah, sorry Katie, please don't cry." Katie looked up and smiled at the girls as she dried her tears.

Ms. PomPom was so happy to see that everyone was getting along and accepting Katie. She shouted out, "Ok girls, are you ready to start cheering?"

"Yay!" they all squealed, as they grabbed their pompoms and began shaking them in the air.

The next few weeks went by so fast. Finally it was "game day". B.B. was feeling butterflies tickling his tummy. He couldn't wait to play in his first game. You could feel the excitement in the air as the game was about to begin.

B.B.'s team had the ball first. Little Nicholas, their quarterback, passed the ball to Evan, but he dropped it. As the team huddled up before the next play, Travis shouted at Evan, "Hey four eyes you have to catch the ball!" B.B. glared at Travis and said, "Stop it Travis! Just give him a chance. Remember Coach Kind said we all have to work together to win!"

Time and time again throughout the game little Nicholas would try to pass the ball to Evan and he'd drop it.

B.B. could see that Evan was growing discouraged as they sat on the sideline. He put his arm around Evan and said, "Don't give up Evan! You can do it! I believe in you!" Evan mustered up a smile and said, "Thanks B.B."

Before B.B. knew it the game was just about over and his team was behind. They needed to score a touchdown in order to win the game. As B.B. and his teammates huddled up, B.B. glanced around at them and said, "Come on team, if we work together we can win the game! Let's try this, Nicholas you're going to pass the ball to Evan."

Travis shouted, "No way, he hasn't caught a ball the whole game!" Evan looked at B.B., his eyes as big as saucers and said, "What if I don't catch the ball?" B.B. smiled and said, "You will. I believe in you and so does everyone else, right team!" A smile shined across Evan's face. That was when Travis realized that it's better to encourage and support your teammates rather than bully and pick on them. Travis looked over at Evan and said, "Yeah Evan, you can do it. We'll help you!"

B.B. and his teammates got themselves set into their positions. B.B. looked over and smiled at Evan again as they heard little Nicholas call out, "HIKE", before tossing the ball through the air towards Evan.

Evan stretched his arms out and caught the ball in his hands. A big smile beamed across his face as he tucked the ball in close to his side and began running as fast as he could down the field. B.B. and Travis were running on either side of him blocking the players from the other team so that they couldn't tackle him.

As Evan crossed into the end zone B.B. could hear the roar from the crowd, but there was one voice that seemed to be louder than the others. He smiled when he looked over and realized that it was Katie he heard, waving her pompoms and cheering with all of her might with the rest of the cheering squad.

B.B. rushed over to join his teammates who were giving Evan high fives while screaming and shouting, "Yay! Yippee! Evan you did it! You won the game!" Evan smiled and looked around to all of them and said, "No team, WE did it, we all won!" "WooHoo!" everyone shouted, continuing to jump around and celebrate as B.B. put Evan up on his shoulders and carried him across the field towards the cheering crowd.

Made in the
USA
Middletown, DE